DOVER · THRIFT EDITIONS

The Metamorphoses
Selected Stories in Verse

OVID

DOVER PUBLICATIONS, INC.
Mineola, New York

DOVER THRIFT EDITIONS

GENERAL EDITOR: PAUL NEGRI
EDITOR OF THIS VOLUME: TOM CRAWFORD

Note

Among the most influential poems in Western literature, the *Metamorphoses* of the Roman poet Ovid (43 B.C. – 18 A.D.) have long provided a rich source for the myths and legends of ancient Greece and Rome, as well as inspiration for a host of later authors including Dante, Chaucer, Shakespeare, and Milton. Arranged around the central concept of change or transformation (metamorphosis), these delightful poetic stories explore the nature of divinity and humanity alike, as well as the interaction between the two. Read and enjoyed for two thousand years, the *Metamorphoses* have helped secure Ovid's reputation as one of the greatest of all poets.

Bibliographical Note

This Dover edition, first published in 2003, is an unabridged republication of "Stories from the *Metamorphoses*" (pp. 175–300), from *The Mirror of Venus*, originally published by George Routledge & Sons, Ltd., London, and E.P. Dutton & Co., New York, n.d. The Note has been specially prepared for this edition.

Library of Congress Cataloging-in-Publication Data

Ovid, 43 B.C.-17 or 18 A.D.
    [Metamorphoses. English].
    The metamorphoses : selected stories in verse / Ovid.
        p. cm. — (Dover thrift edition).
    ISBN 0-486-42758-7
        1. Fables, Latin—Translations into English.
    2. Metamorphosis—Mythology—Poetry. 3. Mythology, Classical—Poetry.
    I. Wright, Frederick Adam, 1869-1946. II. Title. III. Dover thrift editions

PA6522.M2 W75 2003
871'.01—dc21

2002041300

Manufactured in the United States of America
Dover Publications, Inc., 31 East 2nd Street, Mineola, N.Y. 11501

APOLLO AND DAPHNE

APOLLO, fresh from slaying the Python with his arrows, mocks at his brother Cupid's puny bow. The little god in revenge fires him with love for Daphne, daughter of the river god Peneus, who rejects his suit, and is by her father changed into a laurel.

THEN from his quiver Cupid took two darts :
One kindles love, one hate in mortal hearts.
The first, sharp-pointed, with a golden head,
The other dull, and blunt, and tipped with lead.
With this he Daphne smote, and then he drew
The golden shaft and pierced Apollo through,
Who straightway burned with passion, while the
    maid
Was of the very name of love afraid.
Within the woods she dwelt, and in her toils
Caught the wild deer, rejoicing in their spoils,
Like chaste Diana with her hair unbound,
Her home the forest brake, her bed the ground.

Full many a lover sought her for his bride ;
But all she drove unheeded from her side,
Impatient of a man, nor cared to know
The joys that Hymen and young Love allow.
Oft would her father say : ' A husband take—
It is your due—and me a grandsire make.'
But still she shrank from wedlock as a thing
Of evil concupiscence and would fling
Her arms about him and with burning face
In coaxing guise would ask him thus for grace :—
' As Jove Diana, so permit thou me
To live unwedded and a virgin be.'

But though her father yielded to her prayer,
Her own soft body and her visage fair
Forbade what she desired.   On a day
Apollo saw the maiden, and straightway
Longed to possess her ; and too soon believed
Possession certain, by himself deceived.
As burns the stubble in a corn field dry ;
As hedges blaze, when travellers passing by

METAMORPHOSES

Have built a fire too close or at the dawn
Have left it smouldering ; so the god was thrawn
By fiery passion, and with fancies vain
Must seek at first love's burden to sustain.

He sees her unkempt hair, and fondly cries :—
' What if it were arrayed ? '   He sees her eyes
Gleaming like stars ; he sees her rosy lips
And with another sense would fain eclipse
That lovely vision.   And, while he admires
Her hands and naked arms, his hot desires
Imagine hidden beauties in his dear,
Which when unveiled shall yet more fair appear.

But still she flies him, swifter than the breeze,
Nor cares when Phoebus calls with words like
    these :—

" Stay, river maiden, stay ; I am no foe ;
Not as a wolf do I a lamb pursue,
Nor as an eagle hunts the timid dove :
The cause of my pursuit's not rage, but love.

How do I fear lest in the thorns you fall,
With bleeding limbs, and I be cause of all.
Rash girl, you do not know from whom you fly :
You do not know ; that is the reason why.
Nay, do not run with such excessive speed,
And then I too shall not such effort need.

I am no common swain, nor do I keep
Upon these hills a flock of bleating sheep.
I am the son of the All Highest ; mine
The realm of Patara, and Delphi's shrine,
Claros, and Tenedos : by me men see
What is, what has been, what is yet to be.
By me the lyre responds to tuneful song.
To me the bow and its sure darts belong :
Ah, that Love's shaft more certain than my own,
Has pierced my heart and to my vitals flown.
Throughout the world all herbs obey my call,
Who did invent the art medicinal :
Alas, that love cannot by herbs be healed,
Or those kind drugs that I to men revealed."

METAMORPHOSES

More would he say ; but lo, the timid maid
Fled from his side and left the words unsaid
Yet even than she seemed surpassing fair
As the soft breeze showed all her body bare,
With garments fluttering in the wanton wind,
Her hair unbound and streaming loose behind.
" No more," he cries, " of loving words I'll
    waste."
Flight spurs desire. He follows hot in haste ;
E'en as a greyhound, when a hare's in sight,
Seeks out his prey, while she in headlong flight
Herself seeks safety, and can scarcely know
Whether she be already caught or no ;
So close the muzzle to her flying heels,
So near the fangs that closing round she feels.

Thus ran the god and maid, she sped by fear
And he by hope, on love's wings drawing near,
Nor gave her time for rest, but with hot
    breath
Fanned her loose hair and her white neck
    beneath.

At last her strength was spent, and loud she
  cried,
O'ercome with terror, to her father's tide :—
" Help me, dear father, by thy power divine,
And change the fateful beauty that is mine."
Scarce had she spoken when a torpor fell
Upon her limbs ; a thin and bark-like shell
Begirt her bosom ; where her hair had been
Sprang forth a maze of boughs and foliage green.
Her face, so fair, took on a leafy dress ;
Her flying feet the clinging tree roots press ;
All, all is changed, except her loveliness.

                    Metam., I, 468-552.

METAMORPHOSES

PAN AND SYRINX

Goat-footed Pan, falling enamoured of Syrinx, pursued the reluctant nymph, who, unable to escape from him, in distress called on her river sisters for aid, and was thereupon by them changed into a tuft of reeds. The story is told briefly by Ovid in the Metamorphoses *in his most lively and vivid manner, but, curiously enough, it is made there to serve the purpose of a soporific. Mercury, sent by his father Jove to slay the hundred-eyed Argus and deliver Io from the bondage laid upon her by wrathful Juno, succeeds with this tale in putting the watchful herdsman to sleep, and then kills him.*

THEN spake the god:—"On Arcady's cool heights
Among the nymphs whom Nonacris delights
One naiad was there, Syrinx called by name,
Fairest of all and most renowned in fame.
Oft would she fly the satyrs, when they wooed
    here,
And gods of wood and field who swift pursued
    her ;

For she a virgin was, of Dian's band,
And girt in Dian's fashion well might stand
For Dian's self, save that her bow was made
Of horn, a bow of gold her queen arrayed :
And even thus she was so passing fair
That it was hard to choose between the pair.

One day, as from Lycaeus she came down,
Pan garlanded with spiky pine cone crown
Beheld her and began to woo the maid "—
Here the god stopped nor then to Argus said
How the fair virgin spurned the rustic god,
And flying o'er the wastes by men untrod
Came to the bank where Ladon's waters gleam
And saw her way barred by the sandy stream.
How then she begged the nymphs to change her
    form,
And Pan, who thought to clasp a bosom warm,
Found but a tuft of reeds which to his sighs
Touched by the wind with plaintive note
    replys.

METAMORPHOSES

Nor told he how charmed by the music sweet
Pan cried :—" In union here at least we meet."
And so the pipes unequal, made of reed,
And joined with wax, took then in very deed
The maiden's name, and " syrinx " still are
  called—
All this he said not ; for by sleep enthralled
He saw those Argus eyes fast closed at length,
And took his wand, and with its magic strength
Deepened their slumber, and while fast he slept,
His curved falchion from its sheath he swept,
And smote between the neck and nodding head.
Forth gushed the blood and Argus falls down
  dead,
Staining the rocks with gore : his hundred eyes
Can see no more, and sightless there he lies.

Metam., I, 689-721.

OVID

JUPITER AND CALLISTO

In no legend does the amoral character of the old Greek mythology appear more clearly than in the tale of Jupiter and Callisto. After the great conflagration that follows Phaethon's rash attempt to drive the chariot of the sun, the father of the gods descends to earth to repair the destruction that the fire has caused. He sees there a virgin nymph Callisto, himself assumes the form of her patron goddess Diana, and in this disguise takes advantage of her innocence. She bears a child, but is left by the god to be shamefully expelled from Diana's company, and then by the jealousy of Juno transformed into a she-bear. Only when her son, grown to manhood, is about to kill his own mother in her beast shape does Jupiter intervene and change them both into stars. The story is told by Ovid with his usual light gaiety ; but in itself it is far from being humorous, and is a typical example of those fables that seemed to Plato so objectionable.

METAMORPHOSES

AND now great Jove surveys his walls on high,
If that the fire had marred their symmetry.
But his firm citadel untarnished stands,
And straight he turns his eyes to mortal lands.
First for Arcadia, his chiefest care,
He wakes afresh the streams that scarcely dare
As yet to flow and bids new grass grow green
And verdant forests deck the ravaged scene.
In eager haste he hurries to and fro
Intent upon his kindly task, when lo
He sees a virgin in the Arcadian glade
And burns with sudden passion for the maid.
She was in truth a nymph most wondrous fair ;
No need had she with art to tire her hair
Or spin soft wool to make her raiment fine ;
Her flowing locks one fillet did entwine,
One clasp her tunic fastened when with bow
Or spear in hand she to the chase would go.
Of all the maids on the Maenalian height
None was more pleasing in Diana's sight,
None had more title to the goddess' love,
Ah, that such favours ever fleeting prove !

'Twas midnoon past : the sun in heaven stood
As the nymph came into the virgin wood.
She doffed her arrows, her stout bow unstrung
And on the grassy sward her body flung
Then of her quiver there a pillow made
And wearied slept, alone, yet unafraid.
The god beheld her, as at ease she lay,
And cried, intent at once on amorous play :—
' My wife of my deceit will never know.
But even if she sees me here below
And in her jealous spite begins to bawl,
I shall not care : the wench is worth it all.'

At once he takes the visage and the ways
Of chaste Diana and approaching says :
' Dear nymph, the best beloved of all my train,
Where hast to-day been hunting ?   I am fain
To hear of all thy doings.'   ' Mistress mine,'
Replied the maid, ' I greet thee, queen divine,
Who art to me more mighty e'en than Jove ;
I say it, though he hear me there above.'

METAMORPHOSES

Jove smiled to see himself preferred like this
In woman's guise to Jove, and gave a kiss
More ardent than a girl's ; then, when she tried
To tell her tale, he drew her to his side,
Holding her closely lest she should escape,
And by his acts betrayed his own true shape.

Callisto strove with all a maiden's power—
Juno had been more kind, if at that hour
She had beheld her—but how with a male
Can a girl wrestle or 'gainst Jove prevail ?
The god was victor, and, his triumph won,
Went back to heaven and left the maid undone.

Metam., II, 401-438.

EUROPA AND THE BULL

The various changes of form that Jove assumed in pursuit of his amours are briefly catalogued in the Sixth Book of the Metamorphoses. *Arachne there upon her tapestry tells how the god as an eagle beguiled Asterië, as a swan Leda, as a satyr Antiopë, as Amphitryon Alcmena, as golden rain Danaë, as fire Aegina, as a shepherd Mnemosynë, and as a snake Proserpina. But, strangely enough, none of these stories is taken as the subject for a separate episode in the poem ; and even the tale of Europa, so favourite a subject for sculptors and painters, is scarcely treated with that wealth of pictorial detail which Ovid frequently employs. According to Herodotus, Europa, daughter of Agenor, king of Sidon, was carried off by a Cretan pirate, perhaps the same Captain Bull who seduced Pasiphaë, in revenge for the rape of Io from Argos. But Ovid prefers the more romantic version of the story.*

METAMORPHOSES

THEN did great Jove call Mercury to his side,
And, fain his amorous purpose still to hide,
Said to him : " Son, my dear confederate,
Who on my bidding ever loves to wait,
Go now, and quickly, in your wonted flight
And seek the land that Maia holds in sight
Upon the leftward hand : 'tis Sidon named
By those who dwell within its borders famed.
There you will see along the grassy hill,
The royal cattle, grazing, each his fill.
It is my wish that they should driven be,
Down from their mountain pastures to the sea."

So spake the god ; and soon at his command
He saw the cattle heading to the sand
Along the margin of a sheltered bay,
Where the king's daughter oft was wont to play
With her dear Syrian maids.   He knew full well
That love and dignity can never dwell
For long together or at ease agree ;
And so he laid aside his majesty,

And ceased to be great heaven's almighty god,
Who makes the world to tremble at his nod,
With three-forked lightning and with sceptre
   dread,
But turned himself into a bull instead.

Thus to the royal kine he did repair,
And with them lowed and cropped the grass,
   most fair
Of all the herd ; his skin as white as snow
Untrodden and unmelted, ere it flow
Beneath the rainy south ; his muscles strong
Upon a rounded neck ; his dewlap long ;
His horns, though small, in shape most perfect
   grown
And more transparent than a topaz stone.
Gentle his eyes, not flashing fiercely keen ;
And on his forehead Peace abode serene.

Agenor's daughter looks with wondering eye
On the kind beast ; nor dares at first draw nigh
To touch him, though so placid he appears.
But soon emboldened she forgets her fears,

And gives him flowers to taste.   Presaging bliss
On her white hands he lays a gentle kiss,
And rapt with pleasure scarcely can endure
To check his onset and make triumph sure.
Now he desports upon the grassy plain,
And now, returning to the shore again,
He rolls upon the sand and lets her press
Her hands upon him in a soft caress
And round his horns fresh rosy garlands cast,
Until she climbs upon his back at last,
Unwitting whom she rides.   Then from the
    strand
Slowly the god moves out and leaves the land
And soon, the shallows past, speeds on his way
Across deep ocean carrying his prey.
One hand upon his back, one on his horn
She rests and trembling from the land is borne ;
While as she leaves her native shore behind
Her filmy tunic flutters in the wind.

Metam., II, 836-875.

OVID

DIANA AND ACTAEON

*Actaeon, grandson of Cadmus, king of Thebes,
while wandering in the woods unwittingly dis-
covered Diana at the bath. The goddess in cruel
revenge turned the youth into a stag, and in that
shape he was torn to pieces by his own hounds.*

A VALE Gargaphië lay within that land
  Thick set with pines and dark with cypress
    wood.
And in its depths, not made by craftsman's hand,
  But due to Nature's art, a grotto stood.
For from the living rock and porous stone
She had carved out its arches all alone.

'Twas Dian's sacred haunt, and on one side
  A bubbling spring sent forth a silver wave
Which made a pool with grassy banks set wide
  Wherein the goddess loved her limbs to lave
When she was weary of the sun and heat
And from the chase was fain to make retreat.

METAMORPHOSES

That day into the grotto she did go,
  And gave her armour-bearer there to hold
Her hunting-spear, her quiver, and her bow,
  Its string relaxed, fashioned of shining gold.
One nymph stood helping till she was ungowned,
Two more her sandals from her feet unbound.

Then Theban Crocalë with fingers deft
  Ties in a knot her lady's loosened hair,
Albeit her own to stream at ease is left ;
  While others in their urns fresh water bear ;
Psecas, and Rhanis, and young Hyalë
And with them Nephelë and Phialë.

But as Diana the cool wave was cleaving
  Actaeon wandered through the unknown
    grove
With doubtful steps, his wonted labours leaving,
  And came into the cave. The fates above
Decreed it should be so ; nor did he know
What thing that grotto to his eyes would show.

Loud shrieked the nymphs when they the
    stranger sighted.
  And beating their bare breasts in terror cried
And thronging round their queen, a band
    affrighted,
  Sought from his gaze her nakedness to hide.
But 'twas in vain : the goddess was too tall
And head and shoulders stood above them all.

Red as the clouds upon a summer evening,
  Red as the dawn was fair Diana's cheek
As there she stood, no veils her beauty screening,
  And turning back looked round her shafts to
    seek.
No arrows had she near ; so in their place
She threw bright drops of water in his face.

And as she cast the vengeful stream upon him
  And saw his visage moistened by the foam
She turned again and looking sternly on him
  Spoke him these words in presage of his
    doom :—
" Go—if you can—and say that you have seen
The naked body of the huntress queen."

METAMORPHOSES

No more she said : the water's touch he felt
   And from his head stag's horns at once did
      grow ;
His ears grew sharp, his skin a dappled pelt,
   Arms turned to legs, and hands to hoofs
      below ;
While on his heart a beast-like terror fell
And swift in flight he bounded down the dell.

In a clear pool he sees his transformed face.
   ' Alas ' he tries to say ; but no words come.
A muffled groan of utterance takes the place ;
   And yet his mind remains.   Shall he go home
Or lurk concealed within the forest drear ?
Shame bars the one way and the other fear.

But as he stands perplexed, he sights the hounds
   And flies before those whom so oft he led.
With their fierce baying the wide wood resounds,
   And swift the pack upon their master sped
And tore him limb from limb while all the air
Rang with his cries of terror and despair.

                Metam., III, 155-209.

OVID

SEMELË AND JUNO

Semelë, daughter of Cadmus, beguiled by jealous Juno, prayed her lover Jove to appear before her in his full majesty. Constrained by his oath the god unwillingly consented, and Semelë perished in the overpowering radiance of his divinity. Her unborn child however was taken from her body, and till the due season kept in his father's thigh. The story is interesting, both in itself and as an explanation of the doubtful position held by Dionysus in the divine hierarchy. The son of a god and goddess, Hephaestus, for example, is indisputably a god ; and so also may be the son of a god and a nymph. But the son of a god and a mortal woman is not a god but a hero ; although in exceptional cases, as with Heracles and Aesculapius, he may be taken into heaven. Dionysus is so far unique that his divine father performed for him some of a mother's functions.

METAMORPHOSES

THAT day queen Juno learned a child on earth
Of Jove's own seed was coming quick to birth,
And once again with jealous wrath on fire
Debated how she might assuage her ire.
' Reproaches are in vain with Jove,' she cried :—
' Too oft on him my anger I have tried.
Against the woman rather will I go ;
And if in me men mighty Juno know,
To whom by right is heaven's high command
With starry sceptre in my strong right hand,
Sister and wife of Jove,—a sister true
Though scarce a wife—then yonder wench shall
     rue
This hour, and to me retribution pay.
For 'twas not that in secret love she lay
Or brief her crime : she has surpassed the rest,
And in her body which my spouse caressed
There lies a child conceived, a gift to me
But seldom granted, and she means to be
By Jove a mother, of her beauty vain
Which yet shall be her ruin.   Ne'er again
Call me great Saturn's child unless she fall,
Swift to her doom ; and sent by Jove withal.'

Therewith she rose, and wrapped in golden cloud
Went to the place where Semelë abode.
But first she dimmed the light that from her shone
And changed herself to seem an ancient crone
With wrinkled skin, white hair, and feeble walk,
Bent in each limb, and mumbling in her talk,
In outward shape the very image she
Of Semelë's own nurse, old Beroë.

In parley long the hours sped quickly by
Till to Jove's name they came. Then, with a
   sigh,
" I hope," she said, " that he indeed is Jove,
But yet I fear ; for men are cheats in love
And many a maid, with high flown talk beguiled
Of gods and such like, finds herself with child.
Yet be he very Jove, 'tis not enow.
Let him a proof of his affection show,
And in such splendour come to your embrace.
As when he meets his Juno face to face.
Bid him to don his royal panoply
And let you see him in full majesty."

METAMORPHOSES

Thus did the goddess prompt the guileless maid ;
And Semelë at Jove's next visit said :—
" Grant me a boon nor ask me now to tell
What it may be I deem desirable."
"Have what you will," he cried, " all, all is thine :
Fear not, I swear it by the power divine
Of Stygian streams ; and e'en the sons of heaven
May never break that oath when once 'tis given."

Then answered Semelë, through love too kind
So soon to perish and her death to find
By his compliance :—" As within her bower
Your Juno sees you at love's ritual hour,
So come to me."   Fain had he her forestalled ;
But neither wish nor oath can be recalled.
In deep distress the god to heaven rose
And gathers round about him, as he goes,
The clouds that ever on his frown attend,
Lightnings, and storms, and those fierce winds
    that send
On men destruction, and to end the tale
His thunder and the bolt that ne'er may fail.

Yet, where he can, he lessens his due part
Of majesty, nor takes that potent dart
Wherewith he smote upon Typhöeus' head
And hurled him from the sky, but in its stead
The lighter bolt, which gods ' The Second ' call,
Less wildly blazing and less fierce withal.
Therein arrayed to Agenor's halls he came
And his poor lover.   But no mortal frame
The tumult of his advent could survive
Nor in the glory of his presence live.
Her bridal gift brought death.   The babe
   unborn
By Jove's own hand was from her body torn
And sewn within his thigh, where safe it lay
Till the months passed and came its natal day.

                    Metam., III, 260-312.

NARCISSUS AT THE FOUNTAIN

The nymph Echo, Jove's confederate, after being punished by Juno with the partial loss of speech, fell in love with the boy Narcissus, and when he scorned her faded away into the voice we know. The retribution that came upon Narcissus is told here and by Lord Bacon:—" It fatally so chanced that Narcissus came to a clear fountain, upon the banks whereof he lay him down to repose him in the heat of the day ; and having espied the shadow of his own face in the water was so besotted and ravished with the contemplation and admiration thereof, that he by no means possible could be drawn from beholding his image in this glass ; insomuch that by continually gazing thereupon he pined away to nothing, and was at last turned into a flower of his own name, which appears in the beginning of spring, and is sacred to the infernal powers, Plato, Proserpina and the Furies."

OVID

THERE was a pool with silvery water bright,
　　To which no neat herd e'er his cattle drave;
No she-goats feeding on the mountain height,
　　Nor wandering sheep disturbed the unruffled
　　　　wave.
No bird or beast came near its thirst to fill,
No falling branches broke the mirror still.

Worn with the chase, Narcissus laid him down
　　In the lush grass that grew along the brink,
Beneath the shadow by cool poplars thrown,
　　And stooping o'er the spring prepared to
　　　　drink.
When lo! another beauty met his gaze
That did another thirst within him raise.

For as he bent a wonder came to view:
　　An imaged face that set his heart on fire;
An incorporeal hope, a joy untrue,
　　Shadow of substance, phantom of desire.
Entranced he lies in ecstasy alone
Like some slim statue carved of Parian stone.

METAMORPHOSES

Flung down he marvels at those stars, his eyes,
   And at his locks than Bacchus' own more fair ;
He sees the roses and the ivories
   Of neck and cheek and lips beyond compare.
Now loves he that which others in him love,
And on himself his passion fain would prove.

How often did he stoop to kiss the pool
   That mocked his lips ; how often with his arm
Seek in the depths beneath the surface cool
   To draw towards his lips the shadowed charm.
He knows not what he sees ; but still he burns,
And to the fond illusion still returns.

O foolish boy, why seek to clasp in vain
   A fleeting image !   Nowhere wilt thou find
Thy heart's desire ; nothing will remain
   Shouldst thou endure to leave the pool
     behind.
'Tis but a shade reflected thou dost see,
And if thou turnest 'twill return with thee.

Yet naught could draw him from that lonely
    place,
  No thought of food, or sleep at eventide.
Ever he gazed upon the mirrored face
  And with the vision ne'er was satisfied.
Until at last he rose, and to the trees
Bewailed his mournful fate in words like these :

' Ye woods, where lovers ever shelter find,
  Have you a grief than mine more cruel known,
Or found a heart so vexed by fate unkind
  In all the long years that you here have
    grown ?
I see—yet what I see may not obtain.
I love—and yet deluded love in vain.

And still—O grief !—we are not parted now
  By roads or hills or walls with close shut gates.
If but the water passage would allow
  He too expectant on my coming waits.
For when I stretched my lips towards the spring
He strove to mine his upturned face to bring.

METAMORPHOSES

So slight the barrier that between us lay
  I almost might have touched his rosy cheek.
Come, my beloved, come to me, I pray :
  Fly not from me when I your presence seek.
You need not shun me. I am young and fair
And nymphs have begged me oft their couch to
    share.

Your kindly looks have hope within me bred.
  I stretch my arms ; and you stretch yours to
    mine.
I weep ; you seem at once to droop your head.
  I smile ; your eyes with laughter gayly shine.
And in the movements of your lips I guess
An answer to the words that I address.

Ah ! now I know the truth. I, I am he !
  It is my very self that I desire,
And my own image in the fountain see.
  I lit the flame that burns me with its fire ;
What can I do ? Be lover now or loved ?
Beggared by my own wealth, yet helpless
    proved.

O would that from myself I might escape—
  Strange, strange petition!—Would he were
    not here,
That love of mine, and had another shape
  From that which to my eyes now seems so
    dear.
Full soon, methinks, from this sore load of grief
My very agony will bring relief.

For I must die : and then my pain will end.
  Only I wish that he might longer live.
Two deaths in this one blow will Fortune send
  And to two loving hearts destruction give.
Alas, alas ! I cannot bear my doom :
My life is done ere it had reached its bloom.'

Metam., III, 407-473.

METAMORPHOSES

PYRAMUS AND THISBE

In the ' Pyramus and Thisbe ' Ovid leaves for the moment the romantic legends of gods and heroes, and gives us a simple and instructive tale, explaining the origin of the mulberry's red juice. Of the two hundred and fifty stories in the Metamorphoses *this is the only one that does not appear elsewhere in classical literature, although it was sufficiently familiar to Bottom and his companions. Probably Ovid borrowed it from one of those collections of Eastern tales that afterwards appear in literature as* The Arabian Nights.

In all the East there lived no comelier pair
Than Pyramus and Thisbe, none more fair
In the great city with its walls of clay
Kiln-burnt, where once Semiramis held sway.
Neighbours they dwelt, their houses side by side,
By nearness first and friendship's ties allied
Till years brought love. In truth they would
   have made
A happy couple ; but their sires forbade.

And even then, despite their parents' ire,
Their hearts still burned alike with mutual fire,
Though none would help and looks and gestures
    sad
Were all the food their hidden passion had.

At last they found a chink which none had seen
Within their party-wall—love made them keen
Of vision and to them the hole revealed
Which all the bygone years had lain concealed—
A trusty channel for their speech, where through
Soft words of love might pass and whispers low.
Oft when they stood, thus parted yet so near,
And caught each other's breath with eager ear ;
' O cruel, cruel wall '—they both would sigh,
' Why dost thou still our union deny ?
One fond embrace, how small a thing were this !
Seems it too much ?   Then grant at least one
    kiss ;
And earn our further thanks ; for well we wot,
That 'tis through thee our words have passage
    got.'

So would they talk, and ere ' Good night ' they
    said,
A kiss unfelt upon the wall they laid.

Aurora now had put the stars to flight
And on the herbage dried the hoar-frost white,
When to their chink they came, still grieving sore
And vowed that they could bear their pain no
    more.
' This night,' they whispered, ' while our
    guardians sleep
And all is still, we from the house will creep
Into the open fields about the town
Hard by the mount where Ninus' tomb is
    shown,
And rest in shadow 'neath the mulberry tall
Which stands, with snow-white fruit a mark for
    all,
Beside the running spring.' Such was their plan :
And all too slow that day the long hours ran,
Until at last the sun in Ocean's bed
Sank, and from ocean dark night raised her head.

Then Thisbe oped the door and with veiled face
Went all unnoticed to their trysting-place,
And by the tomb sat down beneath the tree,
Made bold by love.   But in the darkness, see
A lioness, her jaws adrip with blood,
Who to the spring side came and drinking stood.
The maiden looked, and to the cavern sped
Leaving her cloak behind her as she fled.
The beast, with thirst allayed, the garment
    found,
Its owner safe, and dragged it o'er the ground
With bloody jaws and rent it all around.

The youth drew near; and at that grievous sight,
The cloak besmeared with blood, cried loud,
    " This night
Shall bring two lovers to their death, for she
Deserved to live : she died for love of me.
Mine is the fault : why did I bid her come
To face these dangers and to leave her home
While I was absent ?   Come, ye lions, rend
My guilty limbs as well, and make an end :
Or else this sword upon me death shall send."

METAMORPHOSES

So did he speak, and took the mangled gown
To where the shadow of the tree was thrown.
He kissed the stuff, and cried as his tears fell—
" You shall be reddened by my blood as well ; "
Then at the word drew forth his trusty blade,
And with one thrust an end of living made.
His blood gushed out like water from the main,
When some lead pipe has broken with the strain
And lets the captive stream to heaven rise,
Escaping from the hissing orifice.
The tree ensanguined with the crimson dye
Was reddened to its roots ; and that is why
Still runs with blood the juice of mulberry.

Metam., IV, 55-127.

OVID

SALMACIS AND HERMAPHRODITUS

Hermaphroditus, son of Hermes and Aphrodite, possessed his father's youthful grace, his mother's invincible charm. The naiad Salmacis, living in wanton idleness, fell enamoured of him, and in answer to her prayer was united with him in one body, becoming the sexless bi-sexed creature that we call hermaphrodite. From this story come many of the more voluptuous passages in Shakespeare's 'Venus and Adonis,' although the language of the Roman poet is far less unbridled than that of the Elizabethan.

No spear she ever holds, no painted quiver ;
   Never her time in hunting will she pass ;
She bathes her comely limbs within her river
   And has its water for a looking glass ;
With boxwood comb she combs her flowing
   tresses
And wrapped in lucent robe the herbage presses.

METAMORPHOSES

Often she gathers flowers ; and on that day
  With picking posies she beguiled her leisure,
When she beheld the boy, and lo, straightway
  Resolved to take her fill of amorous pleasure.
But first she pranked her dress and smoothed her
    face,
And called to help her all her beauty's grace.

Then thus did she begin : " A god in sooth,
  And if a god, then Cupid here I see !
Happy thy mother and thy sister both,
  Happy the nurse who gave her breast to thee !
But happier far than all thy promised bride
Whom thou shalt deign to welcome to thy side.

If such there be, let mine be stolen joy ;
  If not, let us in wedlock be united."
So spoke the naiad ; but the timid boy
  Blushed rosy red, his innocence despited—
For never yet of wedlock had he dreamed—
And as he blushed to her more lovely seemed.

As ofttimes in a sunny orchard close
  Half hid by leaves ripe apples we espy ;
As painted ivories their whiteness lose ;
  As the moon reddens in the evening sky
When the loud cymbals clash to bring her aid ;
So were the lad's soft cheeks like roses made.

" Give me at least," she cried, " a brother's
    kiss "—
  And sought her arms around his neck to throw.
" Have done," said he, " I love not ways like
    this ;
  Have done, or I will leave this place and you."
The nymph affrighted feigned to go away,
And in a neighbouring thicket hidden lay.

The boy imagined that he was alone,
  And dipped his feet within the lapping wave ;
And stripping naked, now that she was gone,
  Prepared in the cool stream his limbs to lave.
Spellbound the maid upon his beauty looked
With eyes ablaze, and scarce concealment
    brooked.

METAMORPHOSES

Then with clapped hands he plunged into the
    pool
  And with alternate strokes began to swim.
An ivory statue set in crystal cool,
  A lily seems he on the river's brim.
'Victory!' the naiad cries, and diving down
All naked takes the intruder for her own.

In vain he strives : she holds him closely pressed,
  Stealing a kiss meanwhile, with arms thrown
    round him.
Fondly she touches his unwilling breast
  And will not let him go now she has found
    him.
E'en as a serpent in an eagle's hold
Seeks with soft coils her captor to enfold,

And borne aloft entwines his beating wings
  And wraps herself around his claws and head ;
Or e'en as ivy to a tree trunk clings
  Or as a polyp on the ocean's bed
On every side puts greedy suckers out
And holds his prisoner compassed all about.

But yet the stubborn boy denies her will
   Nor can she gain the joy wherefor she craves,
Until at last close fastened to him still
   She draws him down beneath the placid
     waves
And cries : ' Strive as you may, you shall not go.
Join him to me, ye gods, and keep us so.'

Her wish was granted.   Even as she prayed
   A change came over them, by heaven's might,
Of their two forms a single shape was made
   Which did their bodies twain in one unite,
No longer two, a man and woman, deemed ;
Of either sex or neither now they seemed.

Metam., IV, 308-379.

METAMORPHOSES

PERSEUS AND ANDROMEDA

*Andromeda, daughter of the great African chief
Kepf—in Greek, Cepheus—as a punishment for
her mother's boasting, was taken, by order of the
god Ju-Jah Ammon, to the sea-shore, chained to
a rock, and left to be devoured by a sea monster.
There she was seen by Perseus, as he came flying
back to Europe from the ends of the earth with the
head of Medusa, and by him was rescued and
married. The offspring of their union were the
ancestors of the Persian nation; and this tale
was considered by the ingenious Greeks to account
for their swarthy complexions. Andromeda, it
should be remembered, in spite of the representa-
tions of her legend in modern art, was an Ethiopian
and coal-black.*

By god's decree Andromeda must pay
  For her proud mother's boasting : on rough
    stone
Fastened by chains a captive she must stay,
  To a sea monster left as prize alone.
O cruel fate ! O unjust punishment
By ruthless Ammon on the daughter sent !

So fair she seemed that Perseus swiftly flying
　　Thought her a statue carved in marble rare,
Until he saw her in her anguish crying,
　　While the soft wind disported with her hair.
Then was his heart so thrilled with sudden love
That almost he forgot his wings to move.

Swift he came down ; and, standing by the
　　　　maiden,
　　He cried, enraptured by the beauteous sight :
" Not with such chains as these should you be
　　　　laden,
　　But with those bonds that lovers' hearts unite.
Oh, tell me, pray, your name and your estate,
And why a prisoner by this rock you wait ! "

At first she made no answer to her lover,
　　For she had ne'er been used with men to speak;
And if her hands had not been bound above her
　　She would have sought to hide her blushing
　　　　cheek.
Only her eyes were free ; and these her fears
Veiled in a mist of swiftly-rising tears.

But still he urged her tell him of her sorrow;
  And lest he should imagine she concealed
A crime, from shame some courage she did
     borrow,
  And all her mother's pride to him revealed.
And as she spoke her tale was proven true;
For with a roar the monster swam in view.

Loud wept the virgin when from out the wave
  She saw that grisly head and shoulders rise;
And now her parents, helpless both to save,
  Fill the wide heaven with their woeful cries.
For cries and tears alone were in their power,
Nor could they help their child in that fell hour.

Then spake the stranger: " Time will be
     enow
  For weeping later; 'tis but little space
To aid her that the fates this hour allow.
  Perseus am I; and if you seek my race,
My mother was that prisoner pent in vain
Whom the god filled with seed of golden rain.

The snaky Gorgon's death attests my fame,
  And I have dared on wings the air to ride,
And by my deeds of valour I might claim
  Your daughter, if I asked her, for my bride.
But now, with heaven's favour, I will crown
These with her life, and have her for my own."

(*Then follows the fight between Perseus and the
monster, the hero's triumph, and the creature's
death* (704-734).)

The shores resound with cheers and shouts of
    glee
  And the high hills whereon the great gods
    dwell,
While father Cepheus and Cassiopë
  Salute the hero who has fought so well,
And cry :—' A son indeed to us has come,
The prop and saviour of our royal home.'

The maiden too unfettered shows her face,
  Prize of the feat whereof she was the cause,

METAMORPHOSES

And Perseus longing for his bride's embrace
  To lave his war-worn hands fresh water draws;
And that the Gorgon's head no stones may
    bruise
On the hard sand green leaves and seaweed
    strews.

Then with fresh turf he builds him altars three ;
  The left for Mercury, the next for Jove,
And on the right, Minerva, one for thee,
  Whereon he slays a cow : the king above
Receives an ox, and last he dyes the sod
With bullock's blood to please the wingèd god.

And now the maid as guerdon he can take ;
  Nor wishes he for greater gift withal.
Hymen and Love the marriage torches shake
  And fragrant incense fills the flower-decked
    hall :
While merry songs, the signs of men's delight,
To lyre and flute re-echo through the night.

                Metam., IV, 671-764.

ARETHUSA AND THE RIVER-GOD

The tale of Arethusa and Alpheüs is a very curious example of local legend passing into mythology. In the island of Ortygia, near Syracuse, there was a fountain Arethusa, " the gusher" ; in the Peloponnese on the west coast there was a river Alpheüs. A persistent belief existed that between fountain and river there was an undersea connection, and that any object thrown into Alpheüs would appear again in Arethusa. Hence the fable that in mortal shape the river-god loved the fountain nymph ; that to escape from him she fled across the sea to Sicily, and that following her there he mingles his waters with hers in her new home.

" I was a nymph," fair Arethusa said,
" And in Achaea dwelt, a stalwart maid ;
To hunt and fix the nets my chiefest care,
Heedless of beauty though they called me fair.
My face to me gave nothing but annoy
And that soft talk which other girls enjoy—

METAMORPHOSES

' O what firm limbs, O what a comely frame '—
Brought to my cheeks a blush of rustic shame.
I took no pleasure in such things as these
And thought it was a sin to try and please.

Well I remember yet that summer noon
When, as I wandered through the woods alone,
I sudden came upon a murmuring brook,
So crystal clear that in it you could look
And count each pebble in the depths below,
So placid that it scarcely seemed to flow,
Its sloping banks pleached by the pleasant shade
That silvery willows and green poplars made.

My feet at first, and then my knees, I dipped
In the cool wave, and then my tunic slipped
From off my limbs, and hung it on a tree,
And plunged into the stream as nature free.
I tossed my arms and on the water beat,
Gliding and turning in my safe retreat,
When lo, as deep I sank in water cool,
I heard a sound mysterious in the pool.

I leapt to land, while hoarse Alpheüs cried,
' Go not so soon, O do not leave my tide.
Stay with me, Arethusa ; with me stay.'
Fierce came his voice ; I made no more
    delay,
But naked fled, nor had I time to find
My garments on the bank. He pressed behind
On fire with love, nor heeded my distress
If he could take me in my nakedness.
As doves fly trembling when the hawk they
    view,
So hastened I, and so did he pursue.

Through pathless wastes mid rocks I fled
And over plains and tree-clad mountains sped,
Past Psophis, Elis, and Cyllene's hill,
And Maenala, and Erymanthus chill,
And where Orchomenos lies low in shade ;
His match in running, though I was a maid,
But scarce in strength : with ease he could
    sustain
The course that I must labour to maintain.

METAMORPHOSES

The sun shone bright behind me, and it seemed
His shadow ran in front ; or so I deemed
It in my dread ; a surer cause of fear
His trampling feet and breath as he drew near.
At last forspent I could no more endure
And to Diana cried, my helper sure :—
'Save me, thy nymph, whom oft thou didst allow
To bear thy shafts, thy quiver, and thy bow.'

The goddess heard and from the heavenly height
Cast down a cloud, and hid me from his sight,
So that at fault he quested for his prey
Nor could behold where wrapped in mist I lay,
And ' Arethusa, Arethusa ' cried,
Circling about the place where I did hide.
Ah, how I trembled then ! e'en as poor sheep
Tremble when wolves their ravening vigil keep
Or as a hare that seeks 'neath briars to rest
Nor dares to move, by questing hounds hard
  pressed :
For still he lingered and still watched the place
From whence he saw my feet had left no trace.

Down all my limbs an icy moisture ran,
And wheresoe'er I stepped a pool began,
Made with the drops that from my body fell,
And soon, more swiftly than this tale I tell,
I changed to water ; and the god was fain
To mingle with my waves, a stream again.
But lo ! once more Diana came to aid,
And cleft the earth, and for me passage made
To her Ortygia, land I love so well,
And there, returned to light, in this dear fount
   I dwell."
Metam., V, 577-641.

METAMORPHOSES

TEREUS AND PHILOMELA

The story of Tereus, Procne and Philomela, although extremely repulsive in many of its details, was a great favourite at Athens, where it was held up to girls as a warning against any relations with foreign men. Tereus of Thrace, after marrying Procne of Athens, fell enamoured of her sister Philomela, and, while bringing the girl to visit his wife, took her by force, cut out her tongue to prevent her betraying him, shut her up in a lonely house and pretended that she was dead. Philomela, however, contrived to tell the story of the crime on a piece of woven tapestry which she had conveyed to her sister, and Procne in revenge killed her only child, the boy Itys, and served him to his father as food.   At the end all four characters in this woeful drama were changed into birds, Tereus becoming a hoopoe, Itys a sandpiper, Procne a swallow, and Philomela a nightingale.

FIVE years had passed since Procne first was wed
   When to her lord she spake :—" If any grace
Of love has passed between us in this bed
   Grant me a boon, to see my sister's face.
Go, ask my father that to us she come
A little while ; or let me else go home."

Then Tereus launched his ship, and, sail and oar
   Both aiding, sped upon his watery road,
And reached Piraeus and the Attic shore,
   And entered into Pandion's abode.
He clasped the old king's hand, and spake him
     well
And then began why he had come to tell.

" Your daughter longs her sister, sire, to see,"
   He said ; " and soon she will be safe restored,
If you allow her now to come with me :
   That we will promise." As he said the word
Fair Philomel appeared, rich in her dress,
But richer still in native loveliness.

METAMORPHOSES

So look the nymphs who roam beneath the trees
  Through the green forest or the sprites who
    dwell,
Deep in the water, gliding where they please,
  Whereof fond poets in their verses tell :
Or so would look, if they were e'er arrayed
In splendour as was then the Attic maid.

The sight at once set Tereus' heart aflame.
  E'en as ripe corn or leaves or hay in fire
Are swift consumed away, so on him came
  A burning gust of sudden fierce desire.
Her beauty and his mood swift passion move
For men in Thrace are ever prone to love.

Forthwith he plans her handmaid's help to win
  And to corrupt her trusty nurse with gold
And then by gifts to tempt herself to sin
  Yielding his kingdom that fair maid to hold :
Or else by force to carry her away
And at the price of war cling to his prey.

Fast prisoned is he now in passion's chain
  And there is nothing that he would not dare.
His breast the fires of love can scarce contain
  To break through all delays his only care.
So taking as a cloak his wife's behest
With eager lips he urges her request.

Love makes him eloquent ; but when he pleads
  Most hotly, it is still in Procne's name
He weeps, pretending that her words he heeds ;
  And from his guilt acquires a fairer fame.
Alas for mortal folly ! He doth plan
A crime most foul, yet seems an honest man.

Young Philomela too to go is fain.
  She takes her father's neck within her arm
And whispers :—' Let me see my dear again '—
  Hoping for joy whence naught shall come but
    harm ;
And while she knows not yet of his intent
Seeks to beguile him with soft blandishment.

METAMORPHOSES

Upon her Tereus looks with burning eyes,
  And dreams already of unlawful bliss
When he shall have her body as his prize ;
  While as he sees her fondle him and kiss
He wishes now that he her father were ;
Nor if her father, would the virgin spare.

He finds fresh food and fuel for his lust
  In each embrace she on the king bestows ;
Until at last o'ercome Pandion must
  Yield to the pair, and their request allows.
The hapless maid rejoices to believe
That both have won, who both so soon shall
    grieve.

Now the sun's task was done : his chariot falls
  Down through the West, the while a feast is
    made
And wine flows free within the royal halls,
  Until at last in slumber all are laid :
All save the Thracian ; never can he rest,
So fierce the throb of longing in his breast.

He sees again the maiden's blushing face
  And the quick movement of her slender fingers.
He dreams he holds her in a close embrace
  And on her secret charms in fancy lingers.
All through the night his thoughts keep him
    awake
And from his own desires new fervour take.

So morning came, and on his painted barque
  Fair Philomela stepped to cross the sea,
Swift fell the oars churning the water dark
  Until the shore lay dim upon their lee.
'Hurrah,' cried Tereus; 'we have left the
    land :
I have my wish : she's here beneath my hand.'

Metam., VI, 438-531.

METAMORPHOSES

CEPHALUS AND PROCRIS

There is material for at least two modern novels in the story of Cephalus and Procris, which contains much more of psychological interest, much more of the finer shades of amorous feeling than is usual in Greek mythology. The hero's wonderful hound Lailaps and his magic javelin, which always hit its mark and then returned, are extraneous ornaments : the real basis of the story is purely human, the mutual and ungrounded suspicions of a husband and a wife. The episode of the wife's jealousy of a supposed ' Aura ', aroused by foolish gossip, is told by Ovid both in the Ars Amoris *and in the* Metamorphoses. *Equally romantic is the story of the husband's foolish doubting, as told here by himself.*

Two months it was since Procris was my bride
   When on a morn, as by Hymettus' crest
I spread my nets, Aurora me espied,
   Goddess of dawn in saffron vesture dressed.

She burned with sudden passion, woe the day !
And all unwilling carried me away.

Forgive me, queen ; but I the truth must tell.
　As sure as thou with rosy face dost shine
In that dim land where night and morning dwell,
　Quaffing the nectar's juice with lips divine,
So sure my love for Procris stayed : to her
My every word, my thoughts still constant were.

Of wedlock would I speak, and love's young joy,
　And the warm couch by me so soon forsaken,
Until the goddess cried in sad annoy :—
　" Ingrate, be gone : you'll wish you ne'er had
　　taken
Your Procris for your wife in days to come ;
Get to her now."　And so she sent me home.

But as I went I pondered on her warning
　And feared perchance that Procris too had
　　been
Unfaithful to our troth since that fell morning
　When I was borne away by heaven's queen.

METAMORPHOSES

Her beauty and her youth set me afraid,
Though well I knew she was a modest maid.

I had been absent from her for a season,
    And she from whom I came was light of love.
Fond hearts like mine fear all without a reason
    And I resolved her faithfulness to prove.
I changed my visage, by Aurora's power,
And as a stranger sought our marriage bower.

But when to Athens' sacred town I came
    And saw my home before me safe restored,
Unharmed I found it, chaste and free of blame,
    Yet sad and anxious for its absent lord.
And many a trick and turn must I essay
Before unto my wife I found my way.

Scarce could I bear so basely to deceive her
    When I beheld her fair yet sorrowing face :
I longed without more trial to believe her
    And take her to my arms in fond embrace.
Sad were her looks ; but sadness beauty gave
Such as no other woman e'er shall have.

Fondly she seemed to yearn for the departed,
   Who long had left her to her loneliness :
Yet still my doubts prevailed, and soon I started
   With flattering words a lover's suit to press.
But to my pleas she only made reply :—
" One lord I serve and his alone am I."

Had I been sane such words had been enow ;
   But still to slay my happiness I tried.
I promised on her fortunes to bestow,
   And, when she wavered, in base triumph
     cried :—
" It is no lover, wanton, that you see ;
Your husband knows now your adultery."

No word she spake, but silent in her shame
   Fled from her treacherous spouse and from
     his home,
And hating all men to Diana came
   And with her on the mountain side did roam ;
While I abandoned felt within me burn
Love's fiercest fire and longed for her return.

I sent and craved her pardon and did own
  My cruel sin, and said to gifts so great
I too had yielded and I was alone,
  Until at last she pitied my sad state,
Her shame avenged.   And so I won my wife
Again and lived for years a happy life.

Metam., VII, 700-752.

PHILEMON AND BAUCIS

*Many of the Jewish stories have their analogies
in Greek mythology, and the legend of Philemon
and Baucis offers some curious resemblances to the
tale of Lot and his wife. Jove and Mercury,
visiting the earth, are refused shelter by all the
country-side until they come to the cottage where
old Philemon and Baucis live in contented
poverty. They freely offer the strangers all they
possess, and in return are saved from the destruction
by flood which Jove sends upon their wicked*

*neighbours. Their final happy transformation
into trees concludes the history and is here told.*

ONE goose they had, guard of their poor domain ;
Whom for their guests' delight they would have
 slain.
But he was strong of wing, and they were old
And scarce had strength the fluttering bird to
 hold,
Until at last he seemed for aid to flee
To Jove himself and sheltered by his knee.
' Slay not this bird,'—the king of heaven cried,
' I am great Jove and on this country-side
' Must vengeance take. But you shall feel no
 ill :
' Leave this your house and come to yonder
 hill.'
The aged pair obeyed the god's command,
And taking up their staves with trembling hand
Climbed the long slope.   Soon on the crest they
 stood,
And gazing back beheld a mighty flood

That swept tumultous through the fertile
    plains
So that of all the houses now remains
Only their humble roof. They looked in awe,
Weeping their neighbours' fate ; when lo they
    saw
The cot, which for themselves had been too
    small,
Change shape and grow into a temple tall.
Pillars of stone replace its wooden beams,
The thatch turns yellow and now golden seems,
The doors are rich embossed, and all around
Fair slabs of marble hide the naked ground.
Then said great Jove :—' Goodman and thou
    goodwife,
Ask what you will for this your mortal life ;
It shall be yours.' Philemon took aside
Old Baucis for a while and thus replied :—
' Let us both serve yon temple, she and I ;
' And since we have ever lived in harmony
' Grant at one hour that death to both may come
' And that I never see my dear wife's tomb,

' Nor that it be her lot to build me mine.'
Their prayer was answered, and within the
  shrine
They lived at peace together, and foredone
By years and weakness still in love were one.
At last one evening standing by the door,
As they recalled the bygone days of yore,
Each saw the other take a leafy dress
And felt a growth of bark about them press.
' Farewell, dear mate,' they cried, ' Dear mate,
  farewell : '
And straightway yielded to the magic spell.
Such was their end.   The peasants of that land
Show even now two trees that neighbours stand
With double trunk, and make their humble
  prayer
To good Philemon and good Baucis there.

Metam., VIII, 684-721.

THE PROFITABLE CHILD

The story of Erysichthon and his daughter, although it is linked up with the ancient saga and supplied with divine personages, is in its true nature a pure fantasy and might appear in a collection of fairy tales. The wicked Erysichthon sins against the goddess Ceres by cutting down a sacred oak-tree, and in revenge she summons the demon Hunger from the wastes of Scythia and sends her, a kind of vampire succube, to him in his sleep. As the result he is tormented with an insatiable desire for food, to satisfy which he sells all his ancestral possessions, and at last, as is here related, his daughter. Finally he is reduced to eating his own flesh and dies in agony.

BUT still his rage for eating never ceased
And hunger fierce devoured him unappeased.
To it he gave his house, his lands, his gold :
Only his child remained—and her he sold.

But she rebelled and to the god of sea :—
' Save me,' she cried, ' for my virginity
Thou once didst take, nor let me be a slave
Whom as thy lover thou hast deigned to have.
Her prayer was answered.   As upon the shore
She stood, a change came o'er her : who before
Had been a girl now as a fisher stood
With line and baited angle seeking food.
Her master looked, and to the fisher spake :—
' You who with rod and hook your dinner take,
So may the sea be calm and trustful fish
Come to the bait according to your wish
And never feel the hook until they're laid
Safe at your feet ; tell me where is the maid
Who stood just now with locks dishevelled here ;
For see, her footprints plainly still appear ? '
The girl perceived the power of Neptune's gift
And said :—' Excuse me, sir ; I may not lift
My eyes from off this pool, nor have I seen
Aught but these waves since I've a-fishing been.
So may kind Neptune help me in my art
As it is true that no one in this part

METAMORPHOSES

Of the shore has stood for quite a long time
    back,
No man and certainly no maid, alack.'

The buyer in the fisher's words believed
And left her, by the story quite deceived.
And then her former shape to her returned
And for her father many a fee she earned.
For when he saw that she could change her
    look
From purchasers a cheating price he took.
Now as a mare he sold her to them, now
She was a bird, a fallow-deer, a cow.
And so for many weeks she did supply
Victuals wherewith his greed to satisfy.

Metam., VIII, 843-874.

THE TRANSFORMATION OF DRYOPË

The story of Dryopë is a striking example of the sanctity which Greek religion attached to trees and flowers, and of the retribution which might fall upon any one who even unwittingly did them damage. All trees and shrubs were potentially the abode of a nymph—or rather they were the nymph herself in another guise—and to injure them was to injure the divinity. The tale is told by Iolë, Dryopë's half-sister, to Alcmena, mother of Heracles.

THERE is a lake, with myrtle bushes crowned,
Whose shores soft sloping make a beach around.
Thither my sister came, nor dreamed of harm,
Holding her infant child upon her arm,
A nursling at the breast ; for she had mind
Flowers as a garland for the nymphs to find.
Beside the pool a water lotus grew,
Its blooms, not fruited yet, of every hue

METAMORPHOSES

That Tyrian vats afford : her babe to please
My sister stooped and plucked him some of these.
I in my turn bent down to pluck as well
When, as I looked, from those bright blossoms
    fell
Red drops of blood and through the bush
    hard by
A shudder ran, as though of agony.
For you must know within that bush of old
Fair Lotis refuge took—the tale is told
E'en now by rustic hinds—what time she fled
Priapus : there her human limbs she shed ;
But in the foliage still lives on the same
And still is lotus called by her own name.

But this my sister knew not : so dismayed
To the kind nymphs she for forgiveness prayed
And would have left the place : but to the
    ground
Her feet were rooted by strange fetters bound.
To tear herself away in vain she strove ;
Naught of her body, save her arms, would move.

Her lower limbs by bark are held embraced,
Which slowly climbing rises to her waist,
And when in grief she tries to rend her hair
She finds no locks but only foliage there.
Her babe Amphissos feels his mother's breast
Grow cold and hard, and when to her he pressed
No longer could he draw his milky food.
I saw it all : yet helpless there I stood,
And while I clasped the tree trunk to my side
I longed within that self same bark to hide.

But lo, her husband and her hapless sire
Come, making search, and eagerly inquire
Where Dryopë may be. Naught can I say,
But point towards the lotus. They straightway
Kiss the warm wood, and falling prostrate down
Embrace the roots of her who was their own.
For of my sister naught was now left free
Save her dear face : the rest of her was tree.
Yet from her leaves the tears fell fast like rain
And while her lips as yet unclosed remain

METAMORPHOSES

She poured forth these complaints into the
    air :—
' Believe me now : by all the gods I swear,
I have not merited this dreadful thing :
Guiltless has been my life : this suffering
Is not crime's punishment.   Nay, if I lie
May my green foliage wither, sear and dry,
And I by axes keen in sunder hewn
Be logs upon a fire for burning strewn.
Now take my infant from the boughs that
    were
His mother's arms, and let a nurse have care
To give him milk, and let him come and play
Beneath my spreading leaves, and sadly say,
When he has learned to talk :—" Within this
    tree
My mother lives though she is hid from me."
But bid him fear the waters of the lake
Nor ever from these boughs their blossoms
    break,
But rather think that every coppice hides
A goddess who within its depths abides.

Good-bye, dear husband : if you love your wife,
Save these my branches from the ruthless knife
Nor to my foliage let stray goats come nigh ;
Good-bye, dear father ; sister dear, good-bye !
Alas, no longer to you can I bend ;
You must stretch up and me assistance lend.
Give me my babe to kiss, while yet I may
Feel his dear lips. Ah, no more can I say.
Around my neck a choking grasp I feel,
The coils of bark that now above me steal,
And rob me of my sight with their close bands.
Ah me, I shall not need your loving hands
To close my eyes in death, ah me, ah me ! '
Therewith she ceased to speak, and ceased to be.

Metam., IX, 334-392.

METAMORPHOSES

IPHIS AND IANTHE

Before the birth of Iphis the husband of Telethusa declared that he would not rear a girl child. Pretence accordingly was made that Iphis was a boy. The name, like our Leslie, is of common gender, and on reaching puberty a marriage was arranged with Ianthe, a neighbour's daughter. Telethusa in despair prayed to Isis to change her child's sex, and Iphis by the grace of heaven became in reality a man.

Now thirteen years had passed, and for his son
The father sought a wife in union,
And chose Ianthe, of all maids in Crete
The fairest, for his Iphis bride most meet.
Equal in age, in beauty equal, they
Had shared alike their childhood's tasks and play
And to their virgin hearts alike there came
The throb of love and love's consuming flame.
But not alike their hopes of future joy,
Nor the fond fears that all their thoughts
    employ :

Ianthe dreams of marriage when that she,
Whom still she thinks a man, her man shall be :
But Iphis knows that love for her is vain,
For never shall it full fruition gain ;
Yet by the knowledge feels a fiercer fire,
Maiden for maiden burning with desire.

" Oh, what will be the end ! "—she weeping
  cries,
" Have you no ruth, ye dwellers in the skies,
To send upon me this unnatural grief
So monstrous that it passes men's belief !
I must be strong and banish from my heart
This hopeless love where reason has no part.
Hope begets love and hope keeps love alive
And my own sex of hope must me deprive.
My wishes, true, are granted : God has given
All that I prayed to gain from kindly heaven ;
But nature still forbids, and when I go
To play the husband's part she will say no.
Ianthe will be mine—O fate accurst—
And yet not mine ; mid water I shall thirst.

For how can Hymen bless this manless rite
Where bride meets bride upon the wedding
    night ? "

So would she cry aloud and cry in vain,
The while Ianthe with an equal pain
Desired the nuptial hour when they should meet
And she her lover as a husband greet.
But Telethusa, fearing what she sought,
Reasons of sickness and sad omens brought
Why they should stay unwed, and all things tried
To keep her Iphis from Ianthe's side.
Yet soon the day drew nigh : no more delay
Can Telethusa win the time to stay
When Iphis must be wed ; so with their hair
Loosed from the fillets thus she made her
    prayer :
" Help us, dear Isis, heal our sore distress,
As erst thou didst with saving counsel bless ;
For that my daughter lives the light to see
And I unpunished go is thanks to thee."

Tears followed with her words.   At once bright
  gleams
Shoot from the goddess' horns, her altar seems
To move in presage of a change to come,
And Telethusa went rejoicing home.
For as she left the temple, at her side
Her Iphis walked—but with a longer stride
Than erst she used, and with a darker hue
Upon her cheeks than once her mirror knew.
Her looks less timid seemed, her hair unbound
Less flowing, and in all her limbs was found
More than a woman's strength : in very truth
She who had been a girl was now a youth !
The morning came ; great Juno and her child,
Dan Hymenaeus, with queen Venus smiled
Upon the pair ; and Iphis to his bed,
A stalwart husband, fair Ianthe led.

Metam., IX, 718-797.

METAMORPHOSES

PYGMALION AND THE IMAGE

*The story of Pygmalion, like that of Pyramus, is
probably eastern in origin and is connected with
the island of Cyprus, one of the stepping-stones in
the passage of Aphrodite worship from Asia to
Europe. From Pygmalion and his image descend
Paphos, her son Cinyras, his daughter Myrrha,
and her son Adonis.*

For long Pygmalion lived in single state
Holding the race of womankind in hate,
Until at last by idle fancy led,
An image for himself he fashioned.
Ivory he takes, and thence with happy art
Carves forth a figure, perfect in each part,
More fair than woman ; and his skill to prove
With the white statue falls himself in love.
Art conceals art ; she seems a living maid,
Alert and ready, were she not afraid
To vex her maker, who by love inspired
Is for the sculptured shape with passion fired.

Often he lifts his hands the work to try
If it be breathing flesh or ivory ;
Nor will confess its lips still cold remain
To all his kisses, nor can kiss again.
He speaks soft words, and clasps it to his arm,
Fearing the while lest he should do it harm,
And fondles every limb with loving embrace
   warm.

Soon he brings presents, such as girls delight ;
Pebbles, and rounded shells, and nosegays bright,
A bird, a lily, or a painted ball,
Or amber tears that from the poplars fall.
Draped in soft robes, with rings upon its hands
And necklets round its neck, the statue stands.
With chains and pearls adorned it seems most
   fair,
But yet more comely when body bare
It lies upon a couch all purple spread,
And on soft pillows rests its shapely head,
Called by Pygmalion bride and consort of his
   bed.

Now Venus' feast had come ; and to her shrine
All Cyprus thronged.   The sacrificial kine
With gilded horns before the altar fell,
Where incense breathed on high its magic spell,
And as he threw his offering on the fire
Pygmalion voiced his inmost heart's desire—
" If ye, O gods, can give all things, I pray,
" Give me as wife "—he did not dare to say
" My ivory maid," he only whispered low,
" One like my ivory maid on me bestow."
But golden Venus—for herself was there—
Knew what he meant, and smiling at his prayer
As omen of her favour made the flame
Leap thrice in air.   Pygmalion homeward came
And sought the imaged shape in semblance yet
     the same.

But when he bent and kissed her—lo ! her breast
Seems warm beneath the fingers that caressed
Its ivory smoothness, and his touch obeys
Like wax that softens in the sun's hot rays

Or useful grows by use beneath your hand
And takes whatever shape you may command.
Pygmalion thrilled with joy and doubt and fear,
Testing his hopes upon the image dear.
Yes she was living flesh : her veins pulsed fast
And on real lips his lips were pressed at last.
The maiden felt his kiss, and raised her eyes,
And saw at once her lover and the skies,
While he gives thanks to Venus for his longed
   for prize.

Metam., X, 245-294.

VENUS AND ADONIS

From the story of Venus and Adonis in Ovid, artfully blended with another of his tales, Shakespeare took the framework of his poem. How lavishly he embroidered on his material may be here seen.

ONE day as Cupid Venus kissed, his dart
Unwitting grazed her breast. She felt the
   smart
And pushed her son away ; but lo, the sting
Had deeper gone and soon was festering.
Now for Adon she burns, and cares no more
For high Cythera nor for Paphos shore,
Nor Cnidos, nor the Amathuntian ore.
The sky she leaves and thinks Adonis heaven
And holds him fast nor can from him be riven.
Once she was wont to dally in the shade
And to enhance her beauty by the aid
Of cunning artifice ; but now to please
Her love she roams mid hills and brakes and
   trees,
Like Dian girt to knee with white legs bare,
And tarrs the hounds and hunts the flying hare,
The stag with branching antlers and the doe,
And all such beasts as fly before the foe.
But ravening wolves and lions with red maws,
And boars and bears armed with their sharp-
   ened claws

She shuns, and bids Adonis to beware
If haply for her warnings he have care.
" Be bold against the timid : with the brave
Boldness," she cries, " means danger ; do not
   crave
A glory which may cost too great a price
And at my risk neglect my fond advice.
Be not too rash, nor hasten to engage
Those beasts that nature arms fierce strife to
   wage.
Not youth nor beauty nor the charms of love
Avail rough boars' or lions' hearts to move.
Boars in their tusks have all the lightning's
   fire,
And tawny lions rage with deadly ire.
I fear and hate them both."—The boy asked
   why ;
And in her turn thus Venus made reply—
" Strange is the legend of that ancient sin,
Yet am I fain the story to begin :
But with the chase I have been weary made ;
See, yonder poplar offers his soft shade,

Come let us rest beneath it."—At the word
Within his arms she sank upon the sward,
And while her head upon his bosom fell
Began with frequent kiss her tale to tell.

*(Then follows the long story of Hippomenes and
Atalanta, and how the hero by help of the golden
apples given him by Venus conquered the maiden
in the foot race and won her as his bride : how he
then repaid her with ingratitude and was incited
by her to have union with his wife in the temple
of Cybele, who revenged this profanation by
changing them both into savage lions.)*

So Venus warned her lover, ere she sped
Borne on swan chariot from their grassy bed.
But manly spirits ne'er for warnings care :
His hounds had roused a wild boar from his lair,
Swift following on his trail : the boy in haste
Snatched up his spear and the huge monster
    chased.
One glancing blow he struck as from the wood
The boar broke out, and then no longer stood

The beast with curved snout shook loose the
  spear,
Then charged him as he fled in panic fear.
Deep in his groin his tusk he did ensheath
And on the sand Adonis fell in death.

Metam., X, 525-716

THE DEATH OF ORPHEUS

*The Thracian minstrel Orpheus appears in the
legend under a double aspect. As the devoted
husband he goes down to the nether world and by
the power of song almost succeeds in rescuing his
wife Eurydice from death. But he also appears
as an ascetic and a woman-hater, instructing his
disciples in the rules of monastic chastity. Hence
his painful death at the hands of the Thracian
women.*

WHILE with such strains he drew the trees along
And beasts and rocks alike obeyed his song,
The frenzied dames of Thrace in skins arrayed
Beheld great Orpheus as he music made,
And cried, their tresses on the light wind
  borne,—
' Behold the man who holds us all in scorn.'
One cast a spear against the singer's face :
But it refused to wound, and left no trace
Save one faint mark.   A stone another threw
But it was checked as through the air it flew
By those soft strains where voice and cither meet
And fell in suppliant fashion at his feet.

But not e'en this their passion could restrain.
Rage and mad fury in their bosoms reign :
Which yet would have been stayed by music's
  might
Did not their shouts and beating hands unite
With horn and drum and Berecynthian flute
To drown the melody of Orpheus' lute.
So that the stones no longer felt his spell
And 'neath their furious hail the minstrel fell.

Then did the Maenads drive the birds away
Still rapt by Orpheus' voice, and the array
Of snakes and beasts that as an audience stood,
And dared to dye their hands with his pure
    blood.
Even as sparrows will an owl attack
Caught in the daylight roaming, or a pack
Of hounds within Rome's Amphitheatre grand
About a stag in ravening circle stand.

They hurl against the bard their vine-clad
    wands
Ne'er made for men to use with murderous
    hands :
Clods, sticks, and stones fly fast from every side
And chance real weapons to their rage supplied.
For oxen, as it happed, were ploughing near
And at the sight the husbandmen in fear
Gave o'er their toilsome task and fled away
Leaving their tools all scattered as they lay,
Mattocks, and heavy hoes, and pointed rakes
Which for herself each frenzied Maenad takes.

METAMORPHOSES

First they set hands upon the patient kine
And tear them piecemeal, heads and limbs and
    chine,
And then the bard attack and lay him low
Nor to his cries will any mercy show.
Unheeded now the voice, though ne'er before,
Which had entranced the listening woods of
    yore ;
And through those lips, that rocks and beasts
    obeyed,
His soul, breathed forth, its last faint passage
    made.

Each bird, each wilding creature wept for thee,
Dear Orpheus, every stone and every tree.
And as behind thee they had used to go
So now the woodlands shed their leaves in woe.
With their own tears the rivers ran in flood
And all the nymphs of water and of wood
With hair dishevelled and with sombre dress
Proclaimed to fount and forest their distress.

The limbs were scattered ; but upon its waves
Thy head and lyre the rushing Hebrus saves ;
And as they floated down the friendly tide—
O wondrous tale !—thy lifeless voice replied
To the lyre's loud lament and all around
The banks re-echoed with the mournful sound.

Metam., XI, 1-53.

PELEUS AND THETIS

*The common legend tells how Peleus, son of
Aeacus, prince of Thessaly, was the most pious of
men, and as a reward for his righteousness received
from Zeus the sea goddess Thetis in marriage.
Ovid prefers a different version of the story.*

THERE is a bay on the Thessalian shore
　　That curves in crescent fashion : either head
Runs out to sea, and if there were but more
　　Of water, ships might shelter free from dread ;
So firm its beach that footsteps leave no trace,
So clear of weed that runners there might race.

METAMORPHOSES

Hard by the salt sea grows a myrtle wood
   Thick hung with clustering berries red and
     black,
And mid the foliage a grotto stood
   That neither native grace nor art did lack.
There naked Thetis oft was wont to come,
Borne by a dolphin from her watery home.

And there prince Peleus found her on a day,
   Escaped in slumber from the noontide heat;
And with soft words of homage did essay
   To win her love, and humbly did entreat.
But when his prayers were useless, then at length
He sought to force her to his use by strength.

Swiftly the goddess tried her arts of old,
   Or else he would have worked on her his will.
Now she's a bird, but yet he keeps his hold;
   Now she's a tree, he clasps the tree trunk
     still;
Now as a spotted leopard she doth show;
And Peleus frighted lets the leopard go.

But on the morn he prayed the gods of sea
  With   wine   outpoured,   and   eke   with
    slaughtered sheep,
And with the smoke of incense made his plea,
  So that old Proteus rose from out the deep
And said : " O Peleus, thou shalt win thy bride
And take her as a consort to thy side.

When 'neath the rocky cave she lies in thrall
  To slumber, bind her fast in clinging bands ;
And though a hundred shapes to aid she call
  Heed not her guile, but still with stubborn
    hands
Hold her, until her primal form she wear."
So Proteus spake and plunged beneath the mere.

The sun was sinking low and held the main
  Under his sloping chariot in the west,
When the fair Nereid sought the grot again
  And laid her down where she was wont to rest.
Bold Peleus forward leapt, and flung his arms
In close embrace about her virgin charms.

New shapes she takes, but now he holds her fast
　With hands tight pinioned and her limbs wide
　　thrown;
Until by force subdued she sobs at last;
　" 'Tis heaven's will: have Thetis for your
　　own."
The prince triumphant clasps her as she lies
And gets Achilles on his yielding prize.

Metam., XI, 229-265.

CEYX DROWNED AT SEA

*The tale of King Ceyx and his faithful wife
Alcyone is one of the most pathetic in the* Meta-
morphoses, *and the episode of the tempest is
told with all Ovid's usual skill. In the sequel
Alcyone finds her husband's corpse upon the shore,
and the gods in pity change them both into sea
birds.*

Skill fails and courage yields : each wave
    beneath
Seems now to bring the sure approach of
    death.
Some weep aloud, some sit in silent grief,
Some call upon the gods to send relief,
And with their hands uplifted to the sky
Beg for the burial that the waves deny.
Some think of fathers, and of kinsmen
    some,
Others of children, others of their home
Whereto, alas, they never, nevermore shall
    come.

But Ceyx thinks of his Alcyone ;
Upon his lips there is no one but she.
He longs for her alone, and yet to-day
His heart is glad that she is far away.
How would he love to see his native shore
And turn his eyes towards his home once
    more !

But where he is he knows not ; with such
    might
The billows swell, and heaven is veiled from
    sight
By murky clouds more dark than gloom of
    blackest night.

The furious tempest breaks the swaying mast,
The rudder tears away ; and now at last
One overwhelming wave, as heaven high,
Above all others wins the victory.
Onward it sweeps, by its own fury borne,
Like some huge mountain from its foothills
    torn,
Athos or Pindus, till too monstrous grown
It crashes on the ship, which reeling down
Sinks to the sands below, and leaves its men to
    drown.

Most with their vessel perish in the deep
And ne'er returned to light entombment keep

In ocean's darkness ; those who still survive
To stay afloat on broken wreckage strive.
Ceyx himself instead of sceptre grasps
A shattered spar and calls with panting gasps
Upon his sire for aid, yet calls in vain ;
And, as he breasts the fierce tempestuous main
" Alcyone," he cries, and cries aloud again.

While he has strength to swim 'tis that dear
     name
His pallid lips amid the surges frame,
And to high heaven make their piteous
     prayer—
" Ye cruel waves, my lifeless body bear
To her I long for, that upon the strand
I may be buried by her loving hand."
Such was his final cry ; and when the strife
Of wind and water robbed him of his life
His last low murmur was " Alcyone, my wife."

                              Metam., XI, 537-567.

METAMORPHOSES

THE PALACE OF SLEEP

*After the death of Ceyx, Juno takes compassion on
Alcyone and Morpheus is sent in a dream to tell
the wife of her husband's fate. The episode gives
Ovid opportunity for one of his finest pieces of
imaginative description.*

THERE is a mountain in Cimmeria's lands
　　That holds within its sides a cavern deep.
Sunless at dawn, at noon, at eve it stands
　　The home and hiding-place of laggard sleep.
Soft coiling vapours breathe forth from the
　　　　ground
And veils of darkness cast their shade around.

No wakeful cock upon its murky wall
　　With lifted crest proclaims the rising day;
No hissing geese give out their heedful call;
　　No watch-dog breaks the silence with his bay;
No wolves, no sheep, no human voices rude,
No rustling leaves disturb the quietude.

'Tis the abode of rest.   Dark Lethe's stream
   Invites to slumber, murmuring in the gloom,
With waters that themselves entrancèd seem ;
   And by the entrance countless poppies bloom
From whose rich juices dewy night distils
Sleep, and the earth with drowsy effluence fills.

There is no doorway there whose creaking hinge
   Might intermit the silence as it turns
And on the stillness of the night impinge,
   No porter there his watchful taper burns.
But in the midmost cave is set a bed,
Dark hued and soft and with black covers
   spread.

Thereon the god himself a dreaming lies,
   His limbs relaxed at ease in languorous rest,
While empty visions flit before his eyes
   In endless company about him pressed,
Unnumbered as the sands beside the main,
As leaves upon the trees, as ears of grain.

To him fair Iris came and brushed aside
  The phantom shapes that would have barred
    her way.
Awakened by the gleam the dull god sighed
  And his closed eyes to open did essay.
And scarce at length from his own self set free
He asked :—' Why, maiden, hast thou come to
    me ? '

' O Sleep, thou rest for all things, Sleep most
    kind,
  Balm of the soul,' she said, ' who drivest grief
In flight, and solace for our toils canst find
  So that in thee we ever have relief,
Fashion a dream and let it straightway go
And to Alcyone the shipwreck show."

                    Metam., XI, 592-628.

OVID

THE HOUSE OF RUMOUR

*This is a companion picture to the description
that precedes, and an equally good example of
Ovid's powers of invention. Before the Greek
hosts arrive at Troy, their approach is announced
from Rumour's central exchange.*

THERE is a place 'twixt land and sea and sky
Where close the confines of three empires lie.
Thence all things can be seen both far and near,
And every sound comes to the listening ear.
Dame Rumour dwells upon that mountainside,
Her house with thousand entrances flung wide
And open night and day.   Of noisy brass
Its walls are made and sounds bewildering pass
Backwards and forwards, echoed to and fro,
So that each single word is rendered two.

That house is never silent, never still ;
And yet no noisy shouts its chambers fill.

METAMORPHOSES

But a dull murmur, like the ocean's roar
Reverberating on some distant shore,
Or the last rumblings of the thunder, when
Jove stirs the clouds in heaven to frighten men.
From hall to hall a shifting concourse hies,
Falsehoods and Truths, Imaginings and Lies.
One with vain gossip fills his idle ears,
Another carries forth the tales he hears;
And by repeating make each story grow
Adding a little more than what they know.
Here is Rash Error, here is Fond Belief,
And Foolish Confidence, and Panic Grief,
And Sudden Strife, and Doubtful Whispering:
While Rumour borne aloft on busy wing
Sees all that's done in heaven and earth and sea
And searches the wide world for novelty.

Metam., XII, 39-63.

THE CENTAUR LOVERS

The Twelfth Book of the Metamorphoses *ostensibly treats of the same subject as the* Iliad, *the fighting of the Greek army before Troy. But actually most of the book is occupied by Nestor's long story of the contest between the Centaurs and the Lapithae at the marriage feast at Pirithoüs. The most effective episode in his narrative here follows.*

IF to a Centaur beauty we allow
Then Cyllarus was beautiful, I trow.
His beard was golden-red, just newly grown,
And on his shoulders golden locks hung down.
His face was bright and keen: his stalwart breast,
Shoulders and arms and neck and all the rest
Of man about him by a sculptor's art
Seemed to be fashioned, and the equine part
Was equal thereunto, for Castor meet
If he were all a horse, so for the seat
His back was shaped, so firm the muscles rose
Upon his brawny shoulders as he goes.

METAMORPHOSES

Blacker than pitch was he, yet white of tail
And white legged too.   Full many a female
Of his own race had wooed him, but alone
Hylonomë had won him for her own.
Fairest was she of all the Centaur kind
Who dwell within the forest, fair and kind ;
And by the love which freely she confessed
She, and no other, Cyllarus possessed.

She did not scorn the toilet's artful aid,
So far as toilet suits a Centaur maid.
Oft would she comb her tresses : oft entwine
Roses and violets and rosemarine
About her head, and often would she wear
A wreath of snow-white lilies in her hair.
Twice every day she washed her rosy cheeks
Beside the brook that from the mountain seeks
The plain of Pagasae, and twice did lave
Her comely body in the rippling wave ;
While for her dress with anxious care she chose
The most becoming skins of dappled does.

So Cyllarus and she in equal love
Would rest together and together rove,
United in the woods and in their home,
And now together to the feast had come.
As the fight raged they battled side by side
When lo, a spear—whence thrown I ne'er
  espied—
Pierced through the Centaur's breast, his neck
  beneath,
And touched his heart, and straightway brought
  him death.

His wife drew out the shaft and in her arm
Took his poor body, and with kisses warm
Sought to hold back the life that ebbed away
And with fond hand the rushing blood to stay.
But when she felt that his last breath had fled
And saw her love before her stricken dead
She cried aloud—her words I could not hear—
And flung herself upon the deadly spear.
And so by death united in one place
They lay together in their last embrace.

Metam., XII, 393-428.

METAMORPHOSES

THE CYCLOPS IN LOVE

*The ingenuity of the Alexandrian poets turned the
savage Polyphemus into a love-lorn swain. Ovid
follows them to some extent, but makes the giant
revert to his wonted cruelty. The story is told by
the nymph Galatea, " The milk white maid,"
who, in the arms of Acis, listens to the Cyclops'
song, familiar to English ears in Handel's setting,
and is witness of her lover's death.*

A WEDGE-SHAPED headland runs into the deep,
On either side the billows foam and leap ;
Hither the Cyclops climbed, and had no mind
To tend his sheep who followed close behind,
But careless sat him down. Before his feet
He threw the pine-tree, for a ship's mast meet,
That served him as a staff upon his way,
And on his shepherd's pipe began to play.
Its hundred reeds re-echoed all around,
The mountains and the ocean felt the sound,

And as I lay within my distant cave,
Rocked in my Acis' arms beside the wave,
The song he sang came to me on the breeze,
Still I remember it, in words like these :—

" My Galatea is more white
Than privet flowers, than glass more bright ;
Alders are not so slim and tall,
Or frolic kids so gay withal ;
She is more smooth than sea-worn shells,
More blooming than the meadow dells.

The winter's sun, the summer's shade
Are not so welcome as my maid :
The crystal ice is not so clear,
The plane so noble, fruit so dear.
Sweeter than grapes that ripe have grown,
More soft than curdled milk or down,
More fair than watered gardens she,
If only she were kind to me.

METAMORPHOSES

But Galatea's wilder far
Than untamed cattle ever are,
More false than water, hard than oak,
More boisterous than a rushing brook,
Tougher than vines or willows prove,
And harder than these rocks to move.

More fierce than fire, than the wave
More deaf if you her mercy crave;
A peacock praised is not so vain,
Nor thorns so sharp your flesh to pain;
A she-bear will more pity show,
A trodden snake more grace allow.
And—what is worst of all I find—
She can run swifter than the wind.

And yet if she the truth could guess
She would regret her hastiness,
Herself condemn her coy delay
And beg that I might constant stay;
For on the hills my safe retreat
Knows not of cold nor summer's heat.

Apples, and on each trailing vine
Grapes gold and purple—all are mine
And shall be hers : she may partake
Of berries in the forest brake,
Plums waxen pale and red beside,
If only she will be my bride.
Chestnuts and arbute she shall have
And every tree shall be her slave.

These are my sheep, and there are more
That feed along the hills and shore
And in my cavern have their stall.
Indeed I cannot count them all
If you of me their number ask :
Such reckoning is a poor man's task.
But without telling you can see
How full of milk their udders be.

Come listen to my humble prayer.
For Jupiter I have no care,

METAMORPHOSES

His thunder and his levin brand ;
But as your suppliant now I stand.
And tremble at a Nerëid maid,
I who of heaven was ne'er afraid.

I should not be quite so forlorn
If all men's love you held in scorn.
When you the Cyclops hateful find,
Why to young Acis are you kind ?
He may himself and you delight,
But let him come and test my might
And I will tear his limbs in twain
And scatter them upon your main.

For oh I rage, I boil, I burn !
I know not where my steps to turn.
With wrath and anger I'm possessed.
I feel deep down within my breast
A fierce volcano raging there—
But Galatea does not care ! "

Such was his vain complaints : and then he rose
And even as a bull in frenzy goes
When he has lost his mate and will not stay
But over hills and pastures makes his way,
So did the Cyclops in his fury haste
And coming on as we lay embraced
Expecting nothing less than him to see
He cried :—' This union your last shall be.'

His voice was such as suits a giant's frown.
High Etna shuddered.   I in fear plunged down
Beneath the neighbouring waves.   My Acis flies
And for assistance to his parents cries.
But the fierce Cyclops followed as he fled
And tore a mass of mountain from its bed
And hurled it at him.   One piece of the stone
Fell on my Acis—and his life was done.

Metam., XIII, 778-804.

CIRCË'S VENGEANCE

*One day a fisherman of Euboea named Glaucus
noticed that the fish he had caught and flung on
the grass, after nibbling the herbage came to life
again and leaped into the sea. He himself
tasted the grass with the result that he immedi-
ately turned into a merman and took up his dwel-
ling in deep waters. In his new shape he fell in
love with the maiden Scylla, and on her scorning
his suit swam to Circë's island to ask the witch's
help, with the result that is here told. The name
Scylla means ' a small female dog ', and may in
itself be the origin of the legend.*

AND now the merman swimming through the
   foam
To Circë's magic palaces had come.
Full of wild creatures. First he greeting said
To the sun's daughter, then his prayer he
   made :—
' Take pity on a god, O queen divine,
For you alone can help this love of mine

If of your aid I to you worthy seem.
How great the power of herbs no man, I deem,
Knows more than I, who by their magic power
Was changed into this shape in one brief hour.

Now hear the reason why I seek your aid.
Hard by Messenë's walls I saw a maid,
Scylla her name, and straight enamoured fell.
My promises and prayers I blush to tell,
My flatteries, and how she spurned them all
And forced me thus on your strong might to call.
Give me a charm that shall her rigour bend
Or else some herb of magic potence lend,
Not one to drive this passion from my heart
But which shall force her too to bear her part.'

Then Circë answer made :—' 'Twere better far
To court some maid whose eager passions are
As burning as your own and whose love's fire
Flames with an equal fervour of desire.
You should be wooed, not wooer, and I know
You will be wooed, if you some hope allow.

Have faith in your own beauty. I confess
I, the sun's child, myself a god no less,
In spite of all my powers with herb and song
Ask now no more than that I should belong
To you. Scorn her who scorns, your lover love ;
And so to both alike a just judge prove.'

But Glaucus to her words of love replied :
' Sooner shall foliage grow beneath the tide
And seaweed on the lofty mountain side
Then I forget my Scylla : while she's here,
No other heart than her's can I hold dear.'
He spoke, and Circë with fierce rage was fired.
But since she could not hurt him,—nor desired
For still she loved him—on the girl she turned
The wrath wherewith her jealous hatred burned.

Uncanny herbs of magic strength she flung
Well-pounded in a pot and o'er them sung
A hellish charm ; then donned her bright array
And from her palace hastened on her way,
Leaving the fawning beasts, to Rhegium's shore
That faces Zanclë's rocks. The waves upbore

Her feet as on the rushing tide she trod
And o'er the watery ways she went dry shod.

There was a pool, with banks in crescent round,
Where Scylla ofttimes rest and shelter found
From the hot sky and sea, when in the height
The sun stood burning and with his fierce light
Drove every shade away.   There Circë went
And its cool waves with magic poisons blent,
Scattering the baleful juices she had brewed
From deadly herbs in her dark solitude,
And then in wrath to bring the maiden harm
She muttered three times o'er a ninefold charm.

So when fair Scylla to the water came
And waded in the stream, foul things of shame
Loud-barking fastened on her milk-white waist,
Which she, not knowing they were round her
    placed,
Sought to escape, or from the water fling;
But they from whom she flees still to her cling;
And gazing on her legs with startled eyes
She feels fierce dogs' heads there instead of thighs.

Metam., XIV, 8-67.

POMONA AND VERTUMNUS

The old Roman gods do not lend themselves very readily to poetical treatment. Janus, Flora, Ceres and the rest, are work-a-day divinities, each with his allotted task, as severely practical as were the people who worshipped them. But Ovid does his best, and in the story of Pomona and Vertumnus produces at least a charming fantasy.

WHEN Procas in old Rome held sway
   Of all the nymphs in his broad land
Pomona was most skilled, men say,
   The growth of fruit to understand.
For woods and streams she had no care
But only for her garden fair.

Hence was her name. No spear she bore,
   No javelin ; but a pruning hook
With curvèd blade she ever wore,
   Whose aid to curb the trees she took,
Or set a graft within and so
In old boughs make new juices flow.

Nor did she leave them parched and dry,
　　But to the roots of every tree
A trickling stream she would supply,
　　Making her work her joy to be.
No thought had she of love, but pent
Within her orchard lived content.

The leaping Satyrs oft essayed
　　To win her, and Silvanus too.
Oft the young Fauns their heads arrayed
　　With wreaths of pine-cones came to woo,
And he who does in gardens stand
With sickle armed and phallus wand.

But most of all Vertumnus burned
　　With passion never satisfied.
Into full many a shape he turned
　　That he might reach the maiden's side,
And gazed upon her with fond eyes
In this one or in that disguise.

METAMORPHOSES

Now as a reaper he would come,
  His basket full of ripened ears ;
Now as a mower faring home
  With temples hay-wreathed he appears.
And now a drover he would seem
Fresh from the stabling of his team.

Sometimes as a fruit-picker he
  Would mount the trees on ladder high :
Sometimes a pruner feign to be
  Or a leaf-gatherer's visage try.
A gallant soldier he would look,
A fisherman with rod and hook.

At last one day disguised he came,
  Grey-haired, with coloured snood, and stick,
Seeming a bent and wrinkled dame,
  And begged the nymph her fruit to pick :—
" Your trees ", he said, " most lovely are
" But you are lovelier by far."

Then, gazing at the comely maid
  He kissed her thrice with warmer lips
Than suited with the part he played,
  And on the grass beside her slips.
And as he praised the rosy fruit
Determined now to press his suit.

An elm-tree stood before them there
  Within whose branches did entwine
With purple grapes most wondrous fair
  The clusters of a spreading vine,—
" Were yonder tree unwed," he cried,
" 'Twould be but leaves and naught beside.

" And so the vine which now at rest
  Lies sheltered on her husband's arm,
If she upon the ground were pressed
  Would in the dust lose all her charm.
Why not therefrom example take
And for yourself a marriage make ?

METAMORPHOSES

" Ah, if you only would be kind !
   A thousand suitors even now
Desire in you their bride to find
   Would you to their entreaties bow.
No god in all this Alban land
But burns and longs to claim your hand.

" Shun not these joys, lest late you grieve.
   Be wise and listen to my word :
I love you more than you believe ;
   Take young Vertumnus for your lord.
That is a match you ne'er will rue ;
He will be husband staunch and true.

" He does not roam about the streets
   Nor does he, like your other swains,
Court every maiden that he meets,
   He constant to his home remains.
To none is he more known than me
And for him I give guarantee.

" You are his first and only love,
    To you he will devote his days,
His manly vigour he will prove,
    The native charm of all his ways.
He can assume what shape he will
And all you ask he will fulfil.

" The same delights both of you please
    You can each other's pleasures share.
He ever is the first to seize
    The fruit that is your chiefest care.
And ofttimes comes a-plundering
The gifts that from your bounty spring.

" But nothing now does he require
    Of the sweet herbs your gardens own,
Nor has he of your fruit desire ;
    He longs for you and you alone.
Take pity : think that he is near
And that these are his words you hear.

" Beware too lest your ways offend
  The angry gods, and Nemesis
Upon you retribution send ;
  For Venus hates such pride as this.
There is a tale—I know it well—
Listen : and I that tale will tell."

*(Then follows the story of **Iphis** and **Anaxaretë**, given overleaf ; which proving ineffectual, the god returns to his own shape, and **Pomona**, enchanted by his manly beauty, consents to his love.)*

Vertumnus spoke : yet spoke in vain ;
  And straight put off his woman's guise
And as a youth appeared again.
  Bright as the sun when in the skies
His light has put the clouds to rout
And in full radiance he shines out.

The god was ready force to use :
   No force he needed with those charms.
Pomona, when his form she views,
   Falls of herself into his arms,
And smitten with an equal fire
Answers his love with her desire.

Metam., XIV, 623-771.

THE CRUEL MISTRESS

The tale of cruel Anaxaretë, the girl with the heart of stone, and of her luckless lover's death is pure romance, and belongs to the same family as many of the mediaeval love stories. Ovid tries, not very happily, to connect it with the temple of ' The Peeping Venus' in Cyprus, but really it is of universal application.

A HUMBLE swain once loved a proud princess
Nor dared at first his passion to confess.
But when no reasoning could his pain abate
He came as suppliant to the lady's gate,

METAMORPHOSES

And to her nurse revealed his hopeless love,
And then the other servants sought to move
With soft entreaties.   Letters he would write
And beg that they be brought within her sight
Or else hang tear-wet garlands on her door
And lie stretched low upon the unyielding floor.
But she more cold than stone, more hard than
   steel,
Than waves more fierce, would no compassion
   feel—
And mocked his love with bitter words of scorn
Leaving him in despair, of hope forlorn.

At last the youth no more his pain could bear
And coming cried aloud for her to hear :—
'You are the victor : ne'er again shall I
Annoy you now '—and threw a rope on high
Over the door-posts which he oft had wreathed,
And ere he died this last sad utterance breathed.
'Perchance, O cruel, this poor offering
Of all I have will pleasure to you bring.

Now, now at least, your favour you will show
And to this deed some gratitude allow.
I thought of you alone.' So did he cry
In the last moment of his agony :
Then in the fatal noose he thrust his head
And with his face towards her hung there dead.

The servants bore the body to his home
And when the day of burial was come
His hapless mother led the funeral
With wailings through the city. Therewithal
The princess heard and to her window went
To learn the meaning of that loud lament.
But scarcely had she seen him as he lay
Stretched on the funeral pallet when straightway
Her eyes grew stiff and all the blood ran cold
Within her pulsing veins. A magic hold
Constrained her by the window to remain :
She tried to turn her eyes, but tried in vain,
And all her body changed to that hard stone
Which till that hour had held her heart alone.

Metam., XIV, 699-757.

METAMORPHOSES

THE POWER OF TIME

The narrative of the Metamorphoses *in its later stages becomes more serious and less entertaining. Books Twelve, Thirteen and Fourteen deal chiefly with the Trojan War and the early history of Italy, subjects which Virgil had already treated, and Ovid moves rather uneasily under the shadow of his great predecessor. In the last book of all, he introduces Pythagoras and from the philosopher's long discourse the following is a brief extract.*

FROM the great law of change we are not free
And what we seem to-night we shall not be
Upon to-morrow's dawn.   There was a day
When in our mother's sheltering womb we lay
Mere seeds and hopes of man.   Then nature wrought
With cunning hands and to the sunlight brought
The body pent within the maternal frame
And as a feeble babe to life we came.

OVID

At first upon all fours like beasts we went
And when we tried to walk for guidance leant
On some support and then with trembling knees
Began to toddle in our nurseries.
But soon we were more swift, to manhood
  grown,
And all too quick the middle years had flown
Ere feeble now and with declining strength
Down the hillside we came to age at length.
Time saps our vital force.   Milo grown old
Can scarce endure his muscles to behold
That once with Hercules might well compare
And now hang loose and flabby, soft as air.
And so with Helen beauty swift must pass :
She sees the wrinkles in her looking-glass,
And knows that she is old, and sadly cries :—
' Behold the face that Love twice took for
  prize.'
O envious Age, O great devourer Time,
That mortals perish surely is your crime.
With your sharp tooth you gnaw all things away
And lingering bring them down in slow decay.

                           Metam., XV, 214-236.